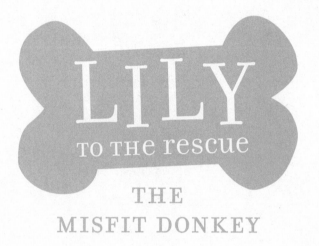

LILY
TO THE rescue

THE
MISFIT DONKEY

W. BRUCE CAMERON

LILY
TO THE rescue

THE
MISFIT DONKEY

Illustrations by
JAMES BERNARDIN

A TOM DOHERTY ASSOCIATES BOOK

NEW YORK

This is a work of fiction. All of the characters, organizations, and events portrayed in this novel are either products of the author's imagination or are used fictitiously.

LILY TO THE RESCUE: THE MISFIT DONKEY

Copyright © 2021 by W. Bruce Cameron

Illustrations © 2021 by James Bernardin

A Starscape Book
Published by Tom Doherty Associates
120 Broadway
New York, NY 10271

www.tor-forge.com

The Library of Congress Cataloging-in-Publication Data
is available upon request.

ISBN 978-1-250-76268-9 (trade paperback)
ISBN 978-1-250-76267-2 (hardcover)
ISBN 978-1-250-76266-5 (ebook)

Our books may be purchased in bulk for promotional, educational, or business use. Please contact your local bookseller or the Macmillan Corporate and Premium Sales Department at 1-800-221-7945, extension 5442, or by email at MacmillanSpecialMarkets@macmillan.com.

First Edition: February 2021

Printed in the United States of America

0 9 8 7 6 5 4 3 2 1

For the wonderful volunteers and staff helping
animals at PAWS Chicago

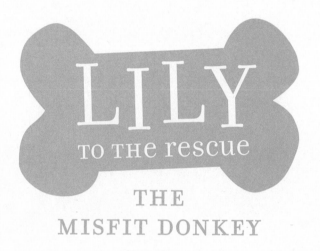

LILY
TO THE rescue

THE
MISFIT DONKEY

Maggie Rose is my girl. I am her dog. In my opinion, this means we should be together every moment. Being together with Maggie Rose means playing with balls in the yard. Or getting belly rubs. (I get the belly rubs, not her.) Or stopping in the kitchen for treats as often as possible.

The kitchen is the best room in the house. It smells amazing. Sometimes I just like to lie on the floor in there and let the smells fill up my nose and hope that soon food will fill up my mouth.

But I can't always be with Maggie Rose, because on some days she says "School" to me and then she goes away. That is very sad. I don't know why a girl would ever go away from her dog.

On those days of "School" I often go with Mom to Work, which is a building full of friends for me to visit. Brewster, one of my very best friends, is an old, tired dog who goes with me on those mornings. Brewster's person is Bryan, who is Maggie Rose's brother. Whatever "School" means, it seems to apply to Bryan as well, because whenever Maggie Rose says it, Bryan leaves, too.

But there are other days that Maggie Rose doesn't say "School," and those are the best days.

On those days, Maggie Rose lies in bed until I jump on her and paw at the blankets and stick my nose under the covers to find her face and lick her ears or her cheek or her chin.

"Lily!" she moans. That's what she did this morning. "Lily! It's Saturday! I wanted to sleep late!"

I understood exactly what she was saying: it was time to wrestle! I grabbed a hank of her hair in my mouth and backed up, shaking my jaws, while she shrieked and giggled. "You are such a crazy dog!"

On this not-School day, Maggie Rose ate toast and other things for breakfast while I sat by her feet and drooled. She saved a crust for me. She always does, and I'm grateful. Maybe someday she will save an entire slice for me. I would be fine with that, too.

Brewster followed me into the kitchen, because Bryan was not home. In fact, Bryan hadn't slept in his bed the night before. I could smell that just as easily as I could smell the fact that Brewster *had* slept in Bryan's bed. Brewster is very good at sleeping on soft things.

Once Maggie Rose and I were done with breakfast, we headed out into the yard. Maggie Rose found one of my toys, one that squeaks in a satisfying way when I bite down hard. She sat down next to me in the grass, holding the toy in one hand. With the other hand, she covered up my eyes.

"Okay, Lily. This is going to be really hard!" she said, and I could feel her move as if she had thrown something. "Find the toy!" she told me. She took her hand away from my face.

I could smell exactly where the toy had landed, so I trotted over to it and jumped on it and chewed it hard, so it squeaked and squeaked and squeaked. I brought it back to Maggie Rose, and she seemed very excited and pleased. Not pleased enough to give me a treat, but still happy.

Brewster was not impressed at all. He just lay in the shade by the fence. I know that he can be lured into playing with a squeaky toy if I jump up and down and shake it right in his face, but it takes a lot of effort.

When Bryan came into the yard, I thought maybe now we'd have a game of two chil-

dren and two dogs and one squeaky toy, but
it didn't happen. Instead, Bryan scuffed his
way across the grass to Brewster, who raised
his head and wagged. You can tell that Bryan
is Brewster's person, because Brewster
doesn't raise his head for anyone else.

"Hi, Bryan!" Maggie Rose called out. "Did
you have a good sleepover?"

Bryan flopped down on the grass and put
his arms around Brewster. I can tell a sad boy
when I see one, and so can Brewster, who

immediately put his head against Bryan's side to give comfort.

Maggie Rose went over to Bryan, so I did, too. Bryan smelled like himself, and Brewster, and peanut butter.

"What's wrong, Bryan?" Maggie Rose asked softly. "Did you and Carter get into a fight?"

Bryan shook his head. Brewster and I looked at each other, wondering what was going on with our people.

"Then what happened?" Maggie Rose asked.

"Carter's moving. To *South Carolina*."

"Oh," Maggie Rose replied.

"He's been my best friend since first grade," Bryan went on. "Then we moved here to this stupid new house, and I didn't get to go to school with him anymore. Mom and Dad said they'd drive me anytime I wanted to see him, but they're always too busy. And now he's the one who's moving, and I'm never going to see him again."

Maggie Rose sat cross-legged in the grass, so I plopped down next to her. Whatever was going on, it seemed like nobody needed a squeaky toy right now.

"I'm sorry, Bryan."

"Now my only friend in the whole world is Brewster."

Brewster perked up his ears. I was sure he could feel the waves of anger and sadness coming off Bryan.

"Well," Maggie Rose began, "you and Carter will still be able to write each other. And FaceTime and stuff. And maybe he could come visit in the summers! I read a book where friends stayed together until they were really, really old, like thirty."

Bryan looked away. "Not the same thing," he replied bitterly.

"So, what about new friends? You could make new friends," Maggie Rose suggested.

Bryan snorted. "Like that's easy. By the time you're in fifth grade, all the kids have best friends already. Nobody needs a new one." He got up. "Come on, Brewster."

I lay next to Maggie Rose as we watched Bryan walk toward the house. They went in the kitchen door. I was worried that he'd get some peanut butter in there and share it with Brewster but not with me. Maggie Rose was worried, too. I could tell.

"We have to come up with some way to help Bryan make friends, Lily," Maggie Rose whispered.

I didn't know what she was saying, so I wagged. Maybe there'd be peanut butter soon.

The next morning, Maggie Rose and I decided that the very first thing we wanted to do when we woke up was to go visit with Mom. Well, actually Maggie Rose decided that, but I was happy to go along. Mom was sitting at the kitchen table eating toast and some other things, too.

I am always glad to eat a crust of toast, no matter who gives it to me. So I sat hopefully at Mom's feet.

"Good morning, Maggie Rose. Want some breakfast?" Mom asked.

"Yes, please, Mom."

Mom stood up and went to the counter and began clinking things together in a way that sounded very much like a good dog was about to get a treat.

"Mom?" Maggie Rose asked. "We're going on our trip today? Just us?"

"That's right!" Mom put bread in the toaster. I wagged at the smell. "Excited?"

"Yes." Maggie Rose nodded. "But . . ."

Mom stopped clinking things and turned. "But what, honey?"

"It's just . . ."

"Just what?"

"Just, whatever we're doing, can Bryan come, too?"

Mom straightened in surprise. "Bryan? I thought you wanted some mother-daughter time."

"It's just that Carter is moving away, and Bryan found out yesterday," Maggie Rose explained in a rush. "So I thought if we're going someplace fun, he'd like to go, and maybe he'd have fun, too."

Mom came back to the table carrying a plate of things that smelled delicious. She placed it in front of Maggie Rose, so I went and sat next to my girl. "Carter's moving away? I didn't know that. That's going to be so tough for Bryan." She sighed. "It's sweet of you to think of inviting him, hon. You've got such a good heart. Yes, I'll ask him. But I don't think we should bring Brewster along on this trip."

"What about Lily?" Maggie Rose asked.

Mom smiled a little. "Lily can come. In fact, it's a particularly good trip for Lily."

"How come?"

"You'll find out. It's a secret." Mom smiled more and took a bite of toast.

I was still sitting and being a good dog when Bryan came shuffling into the kitchen. Bryan always walks as if he's kicking dirt, even if there isn't any. "Where's Craig?" he asked as he sat next to my girl.

"Your brother's already helping your father with chores," Mom replied.

Bryan groaned. "Just great."

I watched them all eat and I noticed that Bryan put peanut butter on his toast. What a wonderful idea! Now we had two kinds of toast right up there on the table. I would love to spend the whole morning tasting first one kind of toast, then the other. We could all do it, and then we'd each decide which was our favorite. My favorite would either be the toast with peanut butter or the toast without.

"Don't you want to do chores today?" Maggie Rose teased him.

"Dad always wants to do chores," Bryan

replied. "If I do them too fast, he gives me more to do, and if I do them too slow, he gives me more to do."

"So . . ." Maggie Rose said slyly, "you want to do something that's not chores?"

"Yeah, of course." Bryan snorted. "Who wouldn't?"

"Like come with me and Mom?"

Bryan hesitated. "Where are you guys going?"

"It's a secret," Mom said, stirring the coffee in her cup.

Bryan frowned. "It's not going shopping for clothes, is it? Like new dresses or something?"

Mom and Maggie Rose both laughed. "No, not that," Mom told him.

"Then what?"

"Come along and find out," Mom told him.

All the people seemed to be having a good time talking. But none of them were saying my name, and none of them were giving me any toast. I flopped to the floor with a long, sad sigh, and just then Bryan flicked a bit of toast off the table. It was a crust with peanut butter on it and it bounced right off my nose! I crunched it right up. My *favorite!*

"Okay," Bryan agreed cautiously. "I'll go."

Then a piece of crust fell from my girl's fingers onto the floor, and I grabbed it just as quickly. It was plain, with no peanut butter. My *favorite!*

"All right, then. Put on some old sneakers, because they might get a little dirty," Mom advised. "Let's go!"

Car ride!

I sat between Maggie Rose and Bryan in the back seat. I licked Maggie Rose and gazed out the window, watching for squirrels. I saw a dog and I barked.

"Lily! Don't bark!" Maggie Rose told me. I felt sure she was telling me I was doing a good job of spotting a dog and barking to let it know I had seen it. The other dog didn't look at me as we went by, probably embarrassed because he didn't have a car of his own. I went back to searching for squirrels.

"Are we going to the zoo?" my girl asked.

"No. Not the zoo," Mom replied. "But there are animals where we're going."

"The game preserve?" Bryan guessed.

"No, not to the game preserve."

"So it has animals, and Lily is allowed to go," Maggie Rose said thoughtfully.

"Oh, I know where we're going!" Bryan announced. "To a farm!"

"Exactly right, Bryan. To a farm where Lily knows two of the animals."

Bryan frowned at my girl. "Lily knows some farm animals, Maggie Rose?"

Maggie Rose shook her head. "I don't think so. Like cows?"

"No, no cows on this farm."

Bryan lifted a hand that smelled marvelously like peanut butter. He scratched his head. "Chickens?"

"No chickens."

"Zebras?" Maggie Rose asked.

Mom laughed.

"Crocodiles? Anteaters? Giraffes?" Bryan guessed. All the humans in the car were laughing, so I wagged. People don't have tails to let others know they're happy, but laughter is the next best thing.

"Oh, *wait*!" Maggie Rose exclaimed. "I know where we're going!"

B ryan was staring at Maggie Rose. "So? Where are we going?" he demanded.

"To visit the pigs!" Maggie Rose replied.

Bryan looked to Mom. "Really?"

Bryan was smiling. It was nice that he was no longer unhappy. I thought of Brewster, at Home, lying on Bryan's bed, believing his boy was still sad. Brewster would be so excited when we returned and his peanut-butter-scented person was cheerful again!

"It's been a little while since we dropped off the piglets at their farm, and I want to check up on them," Mom said. "I try to follow up with all the animals that the rescue places, as best I can. And we don't get too many baby pigs, so I really want to see how Scamper and Dash are doing."

"And that's why Lily gets to come! She's friends with the pigs!"

I knew the word "pig," but could not smell one or see one out the window. It wasn't until the car stopped and the doors opened and I was allowed to jump down that I knew why everyone was talking pigs all of a sudden.

Several smells came to me at once on the warm air. Grass and clover and hay and lots of different animals. I sniffed hard and started to wag, because now I could smell Scamper and Dash!

Scamper and Dash are two pigs who are my friends. A while ago, they came to Work

to drink milk out of bottles and run around like crazy animals. We played and played, and napped, and then Mom or Dad or even Maggie Rose would give them more milk in bottles. But I did not get any of that milk, not even a little bit.

This happens sometimes, but not because everyone loves pigs more than dogs. People just make bad decisions now and then. A good dog has to put up with it, because dogs are better for people than a couple of pigs, even pigs who can run really fast.

I'm sure most dogs would agree with me on this.

I had already forgiven Scamper and Dash for getting bottles of milk when I didn't, so now, I pulled hard against the leash my girl was holding, dragging her toward their smell. We came to a fence made of long wooden rails with spaces between them. Mom and Bryan followed more slowly.

"Okay, okay, Lily, I'm coming!" Maggie Rose said as I towed her. "Wait! Lily, wait!"

I knew she was telling me that she was as excited to see Scamper and Dash as I was.

On the other side of the wooden fence were three big pigs. One of them was very big, and I recognized her scent. She was the mother pig! Her name was Sadie. But where were my little friends Scamper and Dash?

The two pigs that were lying in the muck

with the mother jumped to their feet and ran over to see me at the fence, squealing and kicking up dirt. They shoved their snouts through the fence, and when we touched noses I was amazed.

These big pigs were Scamper and Dash! They used to be babies, and now they were bigger than I was! But they smelled the same, and they were still very friendly. I looked up at Maggie Rose and wiggled impatiently. My girl just *had* to take me off my leash. It was time to play!

She reached down and unclicked my leash. "Okay, Lily!" I dove under the bottom rail of the fence, and Scamper and Dash lunged to greet me. We sniffed each other all over.

Pig is a very interesting smell, not like anything else in the world. It's wonderfully powerful and musty. Once you've smelled pig, you'll never forget it.

So Scamper and Dash were now bigger and

heavier . . . but did they still like to run? I took off at a gallop, looking back in hopes that Scamper and Dash remembered the rules and would follow. They did! My feet splashed and slid in wonderful, slippery, squishy mud, and my two pig friends and I tore up and down their pen together.

The biggest pig lay comfortably in a hollow in the ground where some hay was scattered. Sadie was sort of like Brewster, more interested in lying down than in a wonderful game of Chase-Me. When I ran up to her with my tail wagging, she sniffed my nose gently, but she didn't get up. She was so huge I wasn't actually sure she *could* get up.

That was all right. Scamper and Dash and I were busy enough. I found a scrap of old rope in a corner of the pen and grabbed it with my teeth. I shook it hard and danced with it, teasing Scamper and Dash, but it seems that pigs don't understand how to play Tug-the-Rope. Neither of them tried to grab it.

They did understand Dig, though. When I dropped the rope because I smelled something interesting underneath the dirt, they came to help me claw at the ground. With my paws and their hooves, we sent the dirt flying!

"Lily, yuck!" I heard Maggie Rose call.

I found what I'd sniffed out—it was a big chunk of orange peel that had been squashed into the mud. Then I looked over to see what Maggie Rose wanted.

She was wiping mud off her face and the front of her sweatshirt and shaking her head at me. "You splattered mud all over me, Lily!"

Bryan was laughing at her. "That's what you get for standing too close to the pig pen."

I dashed over to wiggle under the bars of the pen and pant up at her, wagging hard. It was so much fun here! I was glad it was making Bryan and Maggie Rose happy. Then I turned right back to keep on playing with Scamper and Dash.

Out of the corner of my eye I saw my girl stop wiping her face and straighten up. She turned and pointed. "Hey, look!" she exclaimed.

I was very busy with my pig friends. They smelled just like I remembered, and they liked to run just as much as I remembered, but not everything was the same. For one thing, they used to topple over whenever I jumped on them. But now they stayed on all four feet no matter what I did.

I was squirming under Dash's belly when an odd sound filled the air.

It was a low, rumbling noise, deep and loud,

ending in a squeal that reminded me a bit of the sounds Scamper and Dash made. I lifted my head and stared. Trotting up to the fence was what looked a little like a baby horse, but with shorter legs and a thicker body. He stopped and lowered his head to watch me playing in the pen with my pig friends.

"Wow," Bryan said. "It's a baby donkey!"

I decided this new creature might want to play, too! I raced over to the fence to sniff him. He put a furry nose down inside the pen to sniff me back.

I could smell that he was very young. His breath carried the sweet odor of the green grass he had been eating. I sometimes eat grass, too, but only a blade or two at a time. This not-dog, not-horse animal smelled like he never ate anything *but* grass.

I've learned over time that cats and rabbits and weasels and skunks and crows all eat different things, most of it pretty disgust-

ing. They don't know what good dogs know, which is how to sit by a table and wait until toast comes their way—with or without peanut butter. Nothing tastes better than a treat given to me by my girl's hand.

This is something most animals don't seem to care about. If this grass-eating creature was ever lucky enough to be inside the house at dinner time, I bet he would just ignore what was up on the table and hope to be let out to chew on the lawn.

Scamper and Dash charged over to sniff at the new animal's nose through the fence. Maggie Rose came close, too. She reached out and stroked the new animal's muzzle. "I've never seen a baby donkey before. It's so cute!"

A woman I remembered smelling before came over from a house nearby. I wagged in her direction. "That's Burrito," the woman said. "I just picked him up this morning."

She leaned against the fence next to Maggie Rose and Bryan. Mom went over and shook her hand. "Are you Kelly?" Mom asked.

"That'd be me," the woman agreed cheerfully. "You remember me, Maggie Rose? You came with your dad to bring me the little pigs when they were just babies."

I looked at my girl because I'd heard her

name. She nodded. "Is this your donkey?" she asked.

That was the second time my girl had said "donkey." I wondered if the new word had anything to do with this new animal I was sniffing.

"Yes, and he's a sweetie," the woman, Kelly, replied. "Want to give him a treat?"

Treat! Now that's a word that will get a dog's attention. I abandoned Scamper and Dash and squirmed under the fence. The donkey not-dog watched me but didn't change expression or make any noise or wag his tail at all. I did my very best Sit at Maggie Rose's feet to show that I was ready for any treats that might be showing up.

Maggie Rose laughed. "Oh, Lily," she said. "Not for you."

I wagged. *Yes, I am Lily and I am very good and I would like my treat now, please.*

Kelly handed Maggie Rose something. I could smell what it was—a carrot.

I have tried carrots before. They are not too bad, even though you have to chew at them a lot. They come apart in bits, like a squeaky toy. And you can swallow them, just like pieces of a squeaky toy. But they are not treats. So I kept doing Sit, waiting for the real dog treat.

Maggie Rose didn't even seem to notice my good Sit! She held her hand out the way Kelly showed her—flat, with the carrot resting on her palm.

The donkey was very interested in that carrot. He stuck his big nose right into Maggie Rose's hand.

Maggie Rose giggled. "It tickles!" she exclaimed as the donkey crunched up the carrot.

I gave up doing Sit. Nobody was even paying attention, and it wasn't worth doing it for a carrot, anyway. I watched as Bryan held out his peanut-butter-flavored palm with another carrot. That donkey was acting like a carrot was as good as a chicken treat. Donkeys must not be as smart as dogs. Any dog would know that a carrot is not that exciting.

Kelly rubbed the donkey behind the ears. I like getting scratched there, too, so I went up to Maggie Rose and nudged her hand. She had forgotten my treat, but she could give me a scratch at least.

She did.

"I love donkeys," said Kelly. "I had one for years—Mr. Jack. But he died last winter."

"Oh dear, I'm sorry," said Mom.

"That's too bad," Bryan said.

"He had a good long life," Kelly said. "I finally decided I was ready for a new donkey, and I got this one from a farm down the way. I named him Burrito because a *burro* is a small donkey, and he's just a little guy. I figured a little *burro* should be a Burrito! He's kind of shy, but I'm hoping he'll get along with the other animals. The pigs really seem to like him. They were all playing in the big field together this morning. Let's try it again."

She climbed over the fence and opened up a gate to the pigs' pen.

Scamper and Dash squealed with excitement and darted through the gate so fast they nearly knocked Kelly over.

The donkey seemed just as happy. He kicked out his back legs and shook his head and then he ran across the grass, snorting and making more of those loud, funny noises.

Scamper and Dash raced behind him.

Chase-Me! They were doing Chase-Me! I know a lot of games—I can play It's-My-Ball-Not-Yours and Let's-Carry-a-Stick and Dig-in-the-Dirt. But of all games, Chase-Me is the best. I did not want to be left behind, so I ran after Scamper and Dash and the donkey.

"Go, Lily!" Maggie Rose called.

I loved the farm!

The pigs and I ran until we felt like rolling, and then we rolled on the ground in one big pile. The donkey came trotting up to us and flopped down, too, and we all rolled. It was so much fun!

Then I stood up and shook because of another new odor on the air. The farm was full of them!

I turned and saw two boys, one about my girl's size and one much bigger. They were coming up the road, and they were leading a strange animal by a leash that connected to a harness around his head.

I had met this animal before.

5

I heard the new woman, Kelly, say, "Oh, look, here comes Ringo! Doesn't he look handsome!"

The new arrival was a little like a horse, but he had a much longer neck and a smaller head. His fur was fuzzy and looked soft. His head was up so high, it was taller than even the taller of the two boys.

We get a lot of animals coming and going at Work, but this one was one of the strangest-looking. I was about to trot over to greet it and the new boys, but Maggie Rose called me and I went to her side, since that's what good dogs do.

"Is that a llama?" Bryan asked.

"Yep. Name's Ringo. Would you like to pet him? He was over at the neighbor's place, getting his coat groomed," Kelly replied.

"I saw him when I was here before. He didn't want to play with Lily," Maggie Rose added.

Kelly waved her hand. "Let Ringo loose, boys! And come on over."

The taller boy unclipped the horse-thing's leash and it immediately trotted over to where Scamper, Dash, and the donkey were still wrestling in the grass. All three stopped playing to see what this new animal would do.

The horse-thing ignored the pigs. It came right toward the little donkey, stamping with its hard hooves.

"Oh no!" Maggie Rose cried.

She was unhappy. And the little donkey scrambled to his feet and backed away from the big horse-thing. I could tell something was wrong. My new friend was in danger!

I broke out of Sit and raced across the field, coming to a stop directly in front of the horse-thing. I barked, letting it know that if it wanted to hurt the donkey, it would have to deal with a dog.

The horse-thing had large dark eyes with very long eyelashes. He blinked and studied me carefully. Then he made the strangest sound I had ever heard an animal make. His mouth stayed closed, but somehow he brayed a little like the donkey and honked a little like a goose and squeaked kind of like my squeaky toy back Home.

Then he spat right at me. Blinking, I backed away. I'd never been spat at before!

I barked again because I couldn't think of what else to do.

The little donkey was just as confused as I was. He ran around behind me and shook his head. Scamper and Dash seemed nervous and turned and fled back through the gate to their pen.

The two boys came running up. The taller one grabbed the harness on the horse-thing and snicked the leash back onto it. He pulled the spitting, moaning creature back while the younger one came up and put his arms around the donkey.

Soon Maggie Rose and Kelly joined us. Kelly was panting a little.

"Lily!" my girl said. Then she put my leash on, so that now there were two of us on leashes. I hoped she understood I had not been a bad dog. I'd just been trying to help my friend.

The donkey was still being hugged by the smaller boy. He had a scent I recognized. I'd met him before.

"Thank you so much, Kurt, for grabbing Ringo. And you, Bobby, for holding on to poor Burrito," Kelly said.

"Mom and Bryan are putting Scamper and Dash back in their pen," Maggie Rose said.

The horse-thing was eyeing me coldly. Then it turned its head and stared at the donkey. Who would want such a mean thing as a pet? Maybe Kelly should come down to Work and meet some nice animals.

"Hi!" the younger boy exclaimed. "You're

the one who brought the pigs, right? You're Maggie?"

"Maggie Rose. I remember you, Bobby," my girl replied. "Let's put Lily and Burrito into the pen with the pigs. They're all friends."

"Good idea," Kelly said. "And Kurt, you keep hold of Ringo."

The tall boy nodded. "He sure doesn't like that donkey," he said.

We went over to where Scamper and Dash were back behind their fence. Kelly opened a gate and the younger boy led the donkey in. My girl unsnapped my leash. I went under the fence because I could tell that's what she wanted, but I stood near the people while the donkey went to lie down with Sadie and her two big baby pigs.

The humans were talking to each other. Because I am a very smart dog, I figured out that the taller boy was Kurt, and the boy Maggie Rose's age was Bobby.

The spitting, moaning, mean horse-thing was called Ringo. He stood near the people while they talked, and I kept an eye on him while he kept an eye on me. If he spat at Maggie Rose, I would have to bite him right on one of his hooves. I didn't really want to do that, so I hoped he would keep his spit to himself.

"Ringo doesn't like Burrito at all!" Kelly said, shaking her head. "It's so strange. I've never seen him behave that aggressively before toward any of my other animals."

"He didn't like Lily very much, either," Maggie Rose added. I wagged at my name.

"I've heard that llamas can be like that," Mom put in. "They might decide that another animal is a threat for no reason anyone can figure out. Can you keep the two of them separated?"

Kelly put both hands in her pockets. "For right now I can. But Ringo really does have to be free to roam around the whole farm. He's like a guard dog—he keeps an eye on all the animals, and he makes a lot of noise if any predators come near. We're right in the mountains, and there are coyotes around."

"That's what our donkeys do on our ranch," Bobby said. "They keep our place safe from predators."

"Donkeys guard the ranch? What do you mean?" my girl asked.

6

I wagged because my girl had said something, even though I hadn't heard my name.

"No, seriously, they really do act like security guards," Bobby insisted.

"It's funny how they go about it," taller-boy Kurt said. "If the donkeys see anything, like a deer passing by, first their ears all go up and point right at it. Like the way we would point our fingers."

Kurt pointed at me, so I did Sit.

"Then they line up," Bobby said.

"Right," Kurt agreed. "Side by side at the fence, they line up and start up braying. That's to let us know there's something out there."

"What happens if it's a mountain lion? Or a bear?" Bryan wanted to know.

"Then they turn around and show their rear ends!" Kurt hooted.

Nobody told me how good my Sit was, so I got up and stretched.

"And that's scary?" Bryan asked, grinning.

"Yeah, actually, because a kick from a donkey can hurt a mountain lion or even kill it. They could give a bear a hard time," Kurt explained. "It never comes to that, though. We had a mountain lion come up to the ranch once, and when the donkeys lined up it took off for the hills."

"That same cougar came sniffing around here, too, and Ringo chased him off," Kelly agreed. "Nobody wants to be stomped by a llama. It would crush a paw."

"So if Ringo stomps on Burrito, he could really get hurt?" Maggie Rose asked in a small voice.

All the people stopped talking. For some reason, they turned to look at Burrito, who was still sleeping with the pigs. I yawned, thinking a nap might be a good idea.

"I think I should never have bought another

donkey," Kelly murmured sadly. "I don't know what I'm going to do now."

"Know what?" Kurt said suddenly. "I'll bet my dad would want Burrito. He was saying just the other day that all our donkeys are getting to be pretty old. Spud's our oldest, and he's more than thirty."

"Your dad would take Burrito? That would be wonderful," Kelly replied. "That would solve all our problems!"

I noticed that everyone was suddenly more cheerful now. I glanced around but didn't see anything that might explain the change, like a toy.

Kelly went into the pen and hooked a rope around Burrito and led him out through the gate. I wiggled out under the fence and my girl put me on a leash.

I realized that Burrito smelled very much the same as Scamper and Dash. There was a donkey smell underneath, one that was all his own, but on top of that smell there was a lot of pig.

"Well, Burrito, let's go next door and see how you like being with a herd of your own kind," Kelly said.

We all went for a walk! Well, not Ringo, who stayed behind so he could glare and spit at everything. The rest of us headed down a road. I was with my girl, who walked next to Bobby, and Kurt was beside Bryan. Mom and Kelly and Burrito were at the rear.

"We're getting some chickens soon," Bobby told Maggie Rose. "Maybe you could come and get eggs sometime!"

"That would be nice," Maggie Rose agreed shyly.

I smelled where we were going long before we got there. The scent of donkey was very strong on the air. There were also other animals, especially horses. Another farm! I couldn't wait to get back Home so Brewster could smell all the new odors on my fur.

We turned up a rutted driveway and I stopped dead in my tracks, because there in the dirt was the most amazing thing I'd ever sniffed.

Poop! But not just any poop. Giant poop! It was a pile of poop bigger than my head! And not dog poop, either. I have smelled plenty of that. This smelled different, sort of grassy. I sniffed deeply and realized that a horse had left this poop here for me.

"Maggie Rose, don't let Lily roll in that!" Mom called. She was farther back, still walking with Burrito and Kelly.

"I'm trying!" Maggie Rose called. She pulled hard on my leash. "Lily, come on! Lily, I said *come!*"

Of course I knew that I should do what my girl said, but really? Leave the horse poop before I'd smelled it all? I wondered if I should take a little taste. I gave it a lick. Not bad!

"Ugh, Lily, stop it!" said Maggie Rose, and she pulled so hard on my leash that I was forced to leave the poop before I was done sniffing.

At the top of the driveway I could see the donkeys, in a big field next to a building. Burrito made a squealing, braying sound, and I realized that he'd noticed the donkeys, too. One of the donkeys brayed back, and they all lined up at the fence to watch us coming. They had big ears that stood straight up on their heads instead of flopping down like most dogs' do. Those ears swung around to point right at us.

Maggie Rose pulled me close on my leash. "They're pointing their ears. Does that mean they're going to try to kick Lily?"

"No, don't worry," Bobby told Maggie Rose. "The donkeys are used to dogs. We've got

three. I think they're most interested in Burrito, actually. I'm going to go get them some treats that they like, and we'll use those to help them get used to Burrito. It's going to work, I'm sure."

"Where's your father?" Kelly asked.

"He rode off to check on our cattle. Once we get Burrito settled in, I'll grab a horse and go and let him know what's going on," Kurt replied. He looked at Bryan. "You want to come along?"

B ryan blinked in surprise. "Oh. Uh, I never rode on a horse before."

"S'okay, I'll put you up on Daisy. She's pretty much the most gentle horse in the world," Kurt replied.

"You should go, Bryan," Maggie Rose said.

Bryan grinned. "Yeah, okay, cool."

Bobby ran toward a house, and the rest of us waited for him to come back. I drank in the smell of the grown-up donkeys that was drifting toward us on the breeze. They were still all watching us, probably amazed at what a good dog I was being.

The door of the house door banged open, and Bobby came charging back out. He had something in his hands that smelled sweet and juicy. Not as sweet and juicy as chicken, though.

"Watermelon!" exclaimed Maggie Rose.

"Donkeys love it," Kurt said. Bobby handed Maggie Rose and Bryan a couple of pieces, but he did not give any to me, even though I was willing to take a bite to see if I liked it.

The grown-up donkeys were very interested in the watermelon. They stretched their necks over the fence and made happy snorting sounds. Maggie Rose and Bryan held out dripping hands and the donkeys gobbled down the slices of wet stuff as if they were treats. I sniffed at some splashes of juice that fell on the dirt at our feet, but didn't lick it.

"Okay!" Kurt said. "Let Burrito in!"

Kelly opened a gate in the fence and led little Burrito into the donkey yard.

The grown-up donkeys all swung around to glare at Burrito. Their ears pointed toward him.

Burrito took a few steps toward the other donkeys. Then he stopped.

I have seen dogs do that, when they want

to play with some new dogs, but they are not sure that the new dogs want to play with them. Burrito was not sure. He was ready to run if he had to.

And he did have to! Two of the donkeys charged right at Burrito, while the other two brayed with their loud, squealing voices. Burrito fled in panic.

"Oh no!" Maggie Rose cried.

I started to dart forward, ready to protect my friend, but my leash stopped me short. Kurt and Bobby ran into the yard, waving their hands. The grown-up donkeys shied away from the boys, while Kelly quickly led Burrito back out to be with us.

"What in the world?" Kelly wondered. "Why did they do that?"

Mom shook her head. "That's not how donkeys normally behave."

I could tell Burrito was sad. His head was low, and he was staring at the other donkeys.

Maggie Rose petted his nose, but it did not seem to cheer him up.

"Poor Burrito," she murmured.

"It's like when you go to a new school and none of the kids like you," Bryan said.

Everyone was quiet for a moment. "I had friends the very first day," Maggie Rose said softly. "You'll make friends, too, Bryan."

Now Bryan seemed as sad as the baby donkey.

Burrito had backed into thick grass. I walked over to him and touched noses with him to help him calm down.

The other donkeys were watching Burrito closely. Every now and then, one stomped in his direction.

This was not fun! I ran in a circle around Burrito to show all the donkeys how we could play if we wanted to. But Burrito did not want to do Chase. He stayed still, watching the other donkeys as closely as they were watching him.

Meanwhile, Maggie Rose was spinning because my leash was wound all around her now. She reached down and unclicked me.

I figured it would not hurt if I went to see the other donkeys, since Burrito wasn't cheering up. I slid in under the fence rail

and trotted up to the grown-up donkeys and lifted my nose.

"Be careful, Lily!" Maggie Rose warned.

One of the big donkeys put her nose down so we could sniff. Then the others did the same thing.

I sniffed all the noses. Then I ran a little

way into the grass and looked back. Did they know what that meant?

They did! One trotted forward. I ran more, and she came after me.

The others seemed to get the idea. They followed, lowering their heads. I ran in a circle, and the donkeys came with me—all but one, a big male. I could smell that he was very old, and maybe (like Brewster) he would rather nap than run. He dropped his head to snatch a mouthful of grass with a dandelion in it.

I looked up and saw the people and Burrito on the other side of the fence. Burrito was watching us run and chase and chew dandelions. But the little donkey was all by himself.

That was sad. I had all these donkeys to play with, and Burrito had nobody. I squirmed back under the fence and ran up to Maggie Rose.

"Good dog, Lily!" she praised.

I love being told "good dog." Next, I hurried over to Burrito.

Burrito put his head down to meet me and sniffed me all over. I thought he probably liked the smell of donkey that was painted on my fur, just as I loved the smell of pig that was painted on his.

"The donkeys are friendly to Lily," Maggie Rose said. "Why don't they like Burrito?"

"I don't know," Mom said, shaking her head. "I really don't know what's going on."

"Lily likes Burrito," Maggie Rose pointed out.

"Poor little Burrito!" Kelly said, stroking Burrito's nose and rubbing him behind his ears. "First Ringo didn't like him, and now these other donkeys don't like him, either. What am I going to do?"

"I guess it's time to go get my dad," Kurt said. He looked at Bryan. "You ready?"

What happened next was something a dog could never understand. Maggie Rose and the boys took me over to another pen, while Kelly and Mom stayed behind with Burrito. I did not slide under the rails of this fence, because there were horses in there.

In my opinion, horses are too big for their own good. A donkey is about the right size to play with, but a horse is gigantic. They have heads that are bigger than some dogs I have known! Why does any animal need a head that big?

And horses don't seem to play much, either. Mostly they just stand and stare, the way Burrito was gazing at the grown-up donkeys. Maybe that means that horses are sad. But if they are, I don't feel sorry for them, because I've never met one who was friendly to a dog. They don't hum and spit, but they're not going to cuddle up with me, either.

I was absolutely astounded when Kurt and Bobby led Bryan over to a horse and, with a heave, helped him climb on the giant beast's back!

I didn't know if I should bark or whine or snarl, so I just watched in amazement. He couldn't be happy up there on such a huge creature's back! But he was grinning down at us.

Then Kurt swung himself up on another

horse. I glanced up at my girl in alarm. Were
we going to get on a horse?

Bobby pulled open a gate and the boys on
their horses stepped through it. I backed
away from those hard hooves.

"It's okay, Lily," Maggie Rose said. I heard
my name and thought she was probably say-

ing she did not understand why her brother and Kurt were sitting on top of horses.

"Takes us about an hour to get out to where my dad's tending to the cattle," Kurt told us.

"We'll be fine," Mom assured him.

"My dad's pretty much an expert on donkeys. He'll figure out what's going on here," Bobby said as the horses turned their big butts toward us and wandered off.

Poor Bryan, stuck up on a horse.

We returned to Mom and Kelly and Burrito. "Maybe your father will have an idea how to introduce Burrito to the other animals that won't cause so much stress," Mom told Bobby.

"Burrito seems really sad," Maggie Rose said. She sat down in the grass with a sigh.

Nobody was very happy. The farm was such a delightful place, with donkeys and big piles of poop. It was too bad there had to be horses around, but I guessed without the

horses, there would not be any horse poop—
and horse poop was pretty amazing. So why
were the humans so quiet? I pushed against
Maggie Rose to soak up the comfort of being
near her.

"Ugh, Lily! You stink!" Maggie Rose said.
"You smell like a donkey!"

I snuggled closer. I knew she was telling
me how much she loved being with me.

Mom leaned down and sniffed. "Actually,
Lily smells like a pig," she said. "Very much
so. Definitely bath time when we get home."

"Oh, Lily, you're going to make me smell
like pig, too." Maggie Rose scratched gently
at the back of my neck.

Then her fingers stopped.

I looked up at her to see why the scratching
was no longer happening.

"Mom," she said. "Mom?"

"What is it, honey?" Mom asked.

"Lily smells like a pig?"

"She really does. Can't you smell it?"

"I sure can," Bobby agreed.

"What if Burrito does, too?" Maggie Rose went on. "He likes to play with the baby pigs. He was playing with them all morning. What if the grown-up donkeys don't like him because he doesn't smell right to them? He's a baby donkey, but he doesn't smell like one!"

Mom blinked. "Maggie Rose, that's an idea!"

"We've got a hose on the side of the house and some shampoo right there," Bobby said. He sounded hopeful.

And then something truly ridiculous happened.

A bath! Maggie Rose gave me a bath!

Sometimes she does this at home, and I do not appreciate it. I only let her because I love her so much. Usually she does it in the tub, and I have to run around the house afterward and roll on all the rugs and carpets until my fur smells right again.

But this time there wasn't even a tub. She tied my leash to a fence and got me wet with water from a hose and rubbed soap into my fur. I wiggled and squirmed and tried to let her know that this was obviously playtime, not bath time.

It looked like Burrito was getting the same treatment. Mom and Kelly held him while Bobby worked soap and water into his skin.

Poor Burrito. First the spitting, moaning horse-creature was angry with him, and then he didn't get to play with the other donkeys, and now a bath! If I could be in charge of farms, there would be no spitting and no moaning and no horses (but still horse poop, of course) and no baths. But dogs don't get to make decisions about things like that, which is very sad.

"Stop wiggling, Lily. You have to get clean!"

Maggie Rose told me, rubbing soap along my back. "No, stop it! No!"

I wish I knew why humans are so fond of that word "No." I have never met a person who didn't say "No!" at one time or another. It never makes anything better.

Finally, Maggie Rose squirted clean wa-ter over me, and I shook and shook until the tags on my collar rang. I looked around for a rug to roll on, but I did not see one. Maggie Rose untied my leash from the fencepost.

It looked like Burrito's bath was over, too. His fur was damp, and he seemed even gloomier than before.

"Well, that's as clean as we're going to get this little guy, I guess," Kelly said.

"Lily's all clean, too!" Maggie Rose beamed. I

gave her a sour look. Why was she so happy? Didn't she realize that I'd just had a bath and it had been dreadful?

"So," Mom said, "let's take Burrito back and see if he's any more welcome, now that he no longer smells like a pig!"

9

Things were looking better. Maggie Rose led me, and Bobby led Burrito, away from the bath area and toward a marvelously fragrant pile of horse poop, so fresh it was buzzing with flies. A quick roll in that, I knew, would get this awful soapy stink off of my fur. And when I was done, Burrito would probably want to take a turn.

"No, Lily!"

That word again, accompanied by a swift

tug on my leash. I didn't even get to put my nose to the dark lumps in the dirt before I was dragged away.

Even though I love my girl, she just doesn't understand some things. Like horse poop.

Soon we were all back at the fence with the older donkeys milling around on the other side. Their ears came up at our approach. Everybody on our side seemed excited and a little nervous. I couldn't tell what the donkeys were feeling, though.

"Okay, let's give it another try," Mom said. She led Burrito on his leash toward the fence. "I hope this works!"

Mom opened the gate and Burrito stepped hesitantly into the donkey yard. He still seemed pretty glum. I thought I knew the reason why—the other donkeys hadn't liked Burrito earlier. And if they didn't like him, they wouldn't play with him. And nothing is fun when there's no playing.

Why was Mom trying this again? Why didn't we all go back to the pigs and wrestle in the mud? Then Burrito and I could both get rid of the bath smells and have some fun with animals that actually *liked* baby donkeys.

Maggie Rose bent down and unsnapped my leash. "Go and help, Lily," she whispered to me.

Since Burrito was still on Mom's leash and couldn't play, I decided to join the grown-up donkeys. They might not like a Burrito very much, but they liked a Lily! I crawled under the fence and dashed up to my donkey friends, ready for fun.

But they did not seem very interested in me. They had all turned to look right at Burrito and Mom. Their ears swiveled toward the littler donkey. The oldest one stomped and let out a challenging bray.

Burrito backed up a few steps. He looked sad and also nervous.

This was silly. I liked to run. The donkeys liked to run. Burrito liked to run. Why didn't we all do some running right now? Why stomp and stare? I jumped and bowed and wagged so that the donkeys would get the message that there was a dog in their yard who was ready for some serious playing.

The donkeys ignored me. The oldest one brayed again, more loudly. He glared at Burrito.

"That's Spud," Bobby called. "He's the most grumpy of them all."

"I don't think this is working," Kelly added. She sounded worried.

Mom shook her head and pulled on Burrito's leash. She led the little donkey back through the gate. "I'm so sorry, Maggie Rose. It was a good idea. I'm surprised that it didn't work."

"Oh, poor Burrito!" Maggie Rose said. She hugged the little donkey's neck.

The bigger donkeys in the field with me seemed to relax once Burrito was on the other side of the fence. I ran in a little circle and back to them. Did they get the hint? Were they ready to do Chase-Me?

It was hard to tell. I ran in a bigger circle so they would definitely be able to see what I wanted.

Two donkeys settled down, grabbing mouthfuls of grass and munching it. But the other two, who seemed younger, lowered their heads and trotted after me. Then, once they got the idea of running into their heads, they decided they liked it! They took off at a gallop,

dashing all the way around the field. They were fast! I could not keep up, although I tried my best.

After a big circle around the fence, we came back to where we had started. I was panting. The two Chase-Me donkeys both sniffed at me, and the big old donkey huffed out a long breath before he went back to munching.

"Spud's not so angry now," Bobby observed.

I glanced over to see Maggie Rose still hugging Burrito. I didn't mind other animals getting affection, as long as they knew Maggie Rose was *my* girl. But I thought she would have more fun if she were with me in the donkey yard. And Burrito was a donkey. He should come and play with the other donkeys.

This farm was wonderful, but it had some very strange rules. Baths for no reason. People stuck up on horses. Nobody allowed to roll in horse poop, which is obviously what it is for. Baby donkeys not allowed to play with grown-up donkeys.

But people make rules and dogs follow them. That's how it has always been, even though the rules might not always make sense.

I wiggled back under the fence and trotted up to Maggie Rose. I sniffed at her shoes and licked her knee.

"Oh, Silly Lily," she said. She reached
down to pat me.

Burrito lowered his nose to touch mine.
I bowed low and wiggled my rump up high.
Then I ran in a circle again.

"Mom, let go of his rope. I think Burrito
wants to play with Lily!"

Burrito did Chase-Me! We didn't get very far, though, before he came to a halt and gazed at me with his big, mournful eyes. But at least he'd tried. He followed me back to my girl, who petted him. Bobby petted him, too.

"Look, Mom!" Maggie Rose said softly. "All the donkeys are watching Lily and Burrito play!"

"They're certainly interested," Mom agreed.

"They're not pointing their ears at us," Bobby said. "See? So they're just watching now."

Kelly put a hand out and stroked Burrito. "Do you think that means they might be getting used to this little guy?"

Burrito was certainly getting a lot of attention from people, but being petted didn't seem to cheer him up the way it would a dog.

"They're seeing that Lily is friends with Burrito," Maggie Rose said. "And they're friends with Lily. So maybe they'll get the idea that Burrito should be their friend, too."

"Maybe," Mom replied thoughtfully.

Maggie Rose shook her head. "No, Mom, it's true. You know how all the animals at the rescue like Lily so much? I bet those big donkeys do, too. And they're thinking that if they like Lily, and Lily likes Burrito, then maybe the baby donkey is okay."

Bobby grinned. "That could be right! Whenever we get a new horse, we put it on one side of the fence and leave the rest of the herd corralled on the other side. That way, they get used to each other with a fence between them. And then my Dad will give apples to the old horses, and an apple to the new one. He'll go back and forth, handing out apples and carrots, and then when he opens the corral, the new horse is accepted as part of the family!"

"Lily! Go back inside with the donkeys!" Maggie Rose urged.

She obviously wanted me to do something, so I did Sit. That didn't seem to be the right thing, though. Maggie Rose went to the fence, patted her legs, and pointed to the place where I'd been crawling under the rails. "Go, Lily!"

I hesitated. "Go" sounded a little like "no." But there was no horse poop around for her to get all worked up again. So maybe she was saying something else. . . .

Maggie Rose pointed under the fence again. I went over to her and sniffed where she was pointing. There was nothing there but the faint smell of me, where I'd crawled under the fence before.

"Play with the donkeys, Lily!"

I didn't know what Maggie Rose wanted, so I decided it was best to do something fun—like play with the donkeys. I wiggled back into their yard and trotted up to the oldest one, doing a play bow. He eyed me suspiciously.

"Go on, Spud! Play with the dog!" Bobby said.

I spun in a circle. The donkey watched. I

bowed again. No reaction. I kicked up grass as I did a short dash around him, and then he and the other old one chased me a short way. They stopped after a few steps, just like Burrito.

Now it was time for me to chase them back! But the two older donkeys were more interested in eating grass. The two younger ones got the idea, though, and they trotted ahead of me a little, while I ran behind their tails.

"Good dog, Lily!" Maggie Rose called.

There are times when "good dog" leads to treats, so I trotted straight to my girl's side. The donkeys followed me as far as the fence.

No treat from my girl, but sometimes being called "good dog" is reward enough.

"Donkeys are watching," Bobby told us.

The bigger donkeys were all gathered at the fence now. Mom picked up Burrito's leash. "Back up, Maggie Rose," Mom said softly. "I don't want you near in case anybody starts kicking."

My girl backed away several steps. She stood very still. Mom led Burrito right up to the fence.

A grasshopper jumped

out of the dirt at my feet, so I chased it and tried to pounce on it with both front paws. It whirred away, and I jumped again, but I didn't catch it. Where had it gone?

I looked around for the grasshopper and noticed what was happening at the fence.

The older donkeys were sniffing Burrito! They had their long necks stretched over the fence and their soft noses were nuzzling at Burrito's face.

Nobody brayed. Nobody stared. Nobody stomped.

Burrito seemed to get a little braver and moved closer. The other donkeys could now sniff all along his neck and back.

Sniffing is the best way to make friends, of course. I've often wondered why people don't sniff each other when they meet. It's one of the many strange things about people. I've seen people shake Bryan's hand up and down, but nobody has ever thought to

grab his fingers and smell them and maybe lick the traces of peanut butter from his skin.

Certainly *I've* licked him. Even when there's no actual peanut butter clinging to his hands, it's a nice thing to do.

Maggie Rose was bouncing up and down

on her toes the way she does when she's really excited. "It's working! It's working!" she said. "They're figuring out that he smells like a donkey now! They like him!"

"I think you're right!" Mom said. She gently tugged on Burrito's leash and led him over to the gate and into the donkey yard. "Come with me, Lily! Come!"

We were all going to get to play together at last?

I dashed through the open gate and up to Mom, who still held Burrito's leash. The other donkeys slowly approached. A few put their big heads down where I could reach them, and there was more sniffing. It must have been nice for the donkeys, being sniffed by a dog.

I was proud to have taught the donkeys how to play Chase-Me and how to greet a stranger by sniffing. They'd learned very well. If I could get Maggie Rose to hand them some chicken treats, they'd probably give up eating grass forever.

The oldest donkey let out a long sigh that made his nostrils flap.

He stretched out his neck and rested his chin on Burrito's back.

Soon all the donkeys were pressed together, sort of like when I take a nap curled up with Brewster and Maggie Rose. Except we always lie down to nap, and the donkeys were still standing up.

"They do that when they're really happy," Bobby said.

Mom and I left the donkey yard, and I went to Maggie Rose.

"What a smart dog you have," Kelly told her.

Eventually the grown-up donkeys wandered off, staying in pairs as they bit at the grass. Soon they were far out in the field. Every one of them.

Except Burrito.

11

Burrito stood without moving, watching the other donkeys. He put his head down to nose at the grass, but he didn't take a bite.

"Burrito's still sad!" Maggie Rose exclaimed.

"Why doesn't he go out into the field with the other donkeys?" Kelly asked.

"He does seem sad. I have no idea why," Mom agreed.

Burrito was standing and staring at

nothing. He seemed really glum. I wondered if anyone had a squeaky toy we could use to liven things up.

"Here comes Dad," Bobby said.

Dad? I knew who Dad was. I looked around, but I could not smell or see Dad. What I did see, though, were three of those ridiculously large horses trotting toward us. Kurt was still stuck on top of one and poor

Bryan was on another, and there was a man with them, and he was stuck, too.

There were three dogs, their tongues all lolling out, running alongside this strange parade. They stopped when the horses did, and then the man figured out how to get off the horse's back. I was very ready to make friends with the dogs, but they followed Kurt and Bryan and the third horse, who all went around the barn and disappeared.

"Afternoon," the man called with a grin as he approached. "How are you, Kelly?"

"Hi, Matthew. This is my friend from the animal rescue, Chelsea, and her daughter, Maggie Rose."

"And the dog is Lily," Bobby added. "Hi, Dad."

I glanced up at Bobby. He'd said "Dad" again. He sure was confused—Dad wasn't here!

"Glad to meet all of you. Your son Bryan is

a good worker, ma'am," the man told Mom. "Helped me move my herd to fresh pasture."

"Bryan?" Mom repeated, surprised. "He's never ridden a horse before."

"Well, he's a natural," the man replied. He smiled at Burrito, who was still standing by himself. "And look at this beauty! Kurt told me your problem with the llama, Kelly. I could have saved you some trouble—donkeys and llamas don't usually get along unless they're raised up together."

"I just wanted him because he was so cute," Kelly replied with a shake of her head.

"Well, I've been thinking I need to get a few young ones. Old Spud's getting on in his years," the man answered. "Be happy to give you what you paid for him."

Bryan came running up, panting and looking excited. "I had so much fun!" he said, grinning. He certainly was happier than he'd been this morning.

The man grinned. "If hard work is your idea of fun, young man, I'd like to have you visit more often."

Bryan nodded. "Kurt said to tell you he's tending to the horses and then he'll feed the dogs their dinner."

I raised my head sharply. *Dogs? Dinner?*

"But Burrito's sad!" Maggie Rose said impatiently.

The man blinked at her. "Sad, you say?"

"Look at him. Even Lily can't cheer him up."

I wagged at my name. If we were talking about dogs and dinner and Lily then things were definitely looking good.

The man and Mom went through the gate and up to Burrito, who didn't wag or lick or greet them in any way.

The man ran his hands up and down the donkey's back and front legs. "Don't see anything wrong, here."

"I'm a veterinarian," Mom said with a nod. "I think he's perfectly healthy. But he does seem depressed."

The man and Mom came back to our side of the fence. I smelled their hands. His carried the odor of horses, some other animals I couldn't identify, and Burrito the donkey. "You just pick him up this morning?" he asked Kelly.

"Yes, and he seemed fine to me then. Very lively when I first saw him," Kelly replied.

The man took off his big hat for a moment, scratching his head. "Then I got nothin'. Usually there's some trouble introducing a new donkey, but if that were the issue, Spud and the others would be right here letting us know it, instead of off in the pasture."

"Maybe he misses his friends," Bryan blurted.

Everyone looked at Bryan, so I did, too.

"It's like when you move to a new place.

You go to school with the other kids, but you miss your old friends," Bryan went on.

Mom reached out and patted Bryan's shoulder gently.

The man raised his eyebrows. "Well, now, maybe you really are a born rancher. Everybody look out there at my donkeys. See anything?"

"They're just eating like always," Bobby replied.

I yawned and scratched my ear with my rear paw.

"I don't know what I'm supposed to see," Mom confessed.

"They're in pairs!" Maggie Rose exclaimed. "See? There's two close together on one side and two close together on the other."

I wagged because Maggie Rose seemed excited.

"That's exactly right, young lady," the man told her with a nod. "Donkeys form what we

call bonded pairs. Not necessarily with a
mate, and not always with a brother or a sis-
ter, but once they've bonded they do everything together."

"When I met Burrito, he was standing
with another one his age!" Kelly exclaimed.

"There you have it," the man replied with
a grin.

"Burrito misses his best friend," Bryan said, nodding.

"Well . . . looks like I'm going to need to go get myself another little donkey," the man observed cheerfully. "Let's load Burrito into the trailer so he can pick out the right one for us." He looked at Bryan. "If it's okay with your mother, you can come along, too. I could use a hand."

Bryan looked at Mom, who smiled. "That's fine with me!" she said.

Soon I watched in utter bafflement as they led Burrito to a big car that was attached to another big car. When it trundled away, I was left with Bobby and my girl and Mom and Kelly. Bryan had gone with the man and Burrito.

Where were they taking the little donkey? And why did he get his own car?

Maggie Rose put my leash back on and we all went for *another* walk to smell the horse poop. What an amazing day!

Bobby remained behind. Maybe he was going to give the other donkeys their baths now. But Kelly walked with us.

We were soon back at the farm where Scamper and Dash lived. I ignored the ugly horse-thing, who glared at me but didn't spit or moan. Mom and Maggie Rose talked with

Kelly for a long time, and they all said "Lily" a lot, which made me sure they were talking about what a good dog I was and how I should be given some treats immediately.

I wiggled into the pen with Scamper and Dash. They were dozing in a heap with their mother, but they were very happy to wake up for a game of Chase-Me that led us through lots of mud puddles. The mud slipped and slid beneath my paws in a wonderful way, and once I flopped down and skidded on my belly right up to the nose of the mother pig.

Sadie opened her eyes and grunted at me, and I licked her nose and ran off to dig in a corner with Scamper and turned up two apple cores. Scamper ate one and I chewed a little on the other until Dash came and took it away, so of course we had to do Chase some more.

While the three of us were busy, the people stood and talked as people do. "Well, I've got to get back to my chores," Kelly told them.

"Thank you for everything, Chelsea. You, too, Maggie Rose."

"And Lily!" my girl said. I glanced at her but then went back to rolling with pigs.

Eventually Maggie Rose called me and put a leash on me and I was taken on yet *another* walk! Truly this was the most astounding day of my life!

I noticed the horse poop as we passed it again, but I wasn't as excited about it this time.

"You were right to suggest we bring Bryan with us," Mom told Maggie Rose as we walked. "He's really having a good time on the ranch."

"And he figured out what was wrong with Burrito!" Maggie Rose reminded her mother.

"Yes, he did. Maggie Rose, you know that there's not anything we can do about his friend Carter moving away. That's how life is sometimes."

Maggie Rose nodded. "I know. It's like

with the rescue, when we get in a kitten and we all love it, but then we find a home for it and it goes away."

"Exactly. Smart girl."

I saw a grasshopper. I didn't know if it was the same one, but I pounced anyway and then it was *gone*. How do they do that?

Soon we were back up at the donkey yard. The old donkeys were still out searching in the grass for something good to eat, but Burrito was close to the fence, prancing and playing with another baby donkey! I wagged excitedly. A new friend!

The man and Bryan were watching the two little donkeys play. The man turned and smiled as we approached. "Welcome back, you two. I'd like you to meet the newest addition to the family. The lighter-colored one is named Taco."

"Burrito and Taco!" Maggie Rose exclaimed happily.

The leash came off with a *snick* and I wriggled excitedly under the fence and ran up to greet the new donkey, who lowered his nose and sniffed. I knew that I must smell of pig a lot, which was a relief. It was much better than smelling of bath.

We played Chase-Me, which seemed pretty much the only game the donkeys knew. I decided that the next time I came, I would bring a ball.

"Lily!" Maggie Rose called. I went to her, wagging. She snicked the leash onto my collar.

"I mean it, Chelsea. I could use all the help I can get, and your son here is a natural on a horse and a good worker to boot," the man was saying. "Plus, my daughter has piano lessons every Saturday morning right down in town. My wife could bring Bryan back with her, and he could spend the day here on the ranch helping out."

"Would something like that interest you, Bryan?" Mom asked.

Bryan's eyes were as wide as his smile. "Yes!"

Everyone seemed so happy, I just had to wag.

"Here she comes now, in fact," the man observed.

I looked up because a car had stopped in

the driveway. The doors opened. A woman carrying a paper bag waved and went into the house, and a girl ran over to us. She had long hair like Maggie Rose, but she was a little older, I thought. She came right to me and petted me, so I liked her immediately. Her pants smelled like peanut butter, and so did her hands.

"Audrey, meet Maggie Rose, and Mrs. Murphy, and Lily. Oh, and this is Bryan."

"Hi," the girl said. "What grade are you in?"

"Fifth grade," Bryan answered.

"I'm in third," Maggie Rose put in.

"I'm in fifth, too," the girl said.

"Bryan's going to come help out every Saturday for a few hours," the man said mildly. "Maybe you could show him the ropes, Audrey."

The girl, Audrey, nodded. "I'd like that," she said simply.

"That's wonderful," said Mom. "Well, we've really got to head home. Maggie Rose, if you don't mind . . ."

"You know what that means, Lily, you piggy-smelling dog," Maggie Rose told me.

I wagged happily up at her. I was sure that whatever was going to happen next, I would really enjoy it. I felt that way as Maggie Rose took my leash. I felt that way as she led me to the side of the house. I even felt that way when she tied my leash to the fence.

But when she turned on the hose, I no longer felt that way.

Baths are the *worst*.

Male donkeys are known as jacks, and female donkeys are jennets or jennies.

In the wild, donkeys live in herds, usually with one male and several females.

Tame donkeys are used to carry loads or to provide milk. Sometimes they also protect other animals on a farm or ranch. They will fight off anything they see as a threat by stomping or kicking.

In the United States, wild donkeys are known as *burros.*

Tame donkeys, like Burrito, usually weigh

between four hundred and five hundred pounds when they are full grown. The largest breed of donkey, called the American Mammoth Jack, can weigh twice as much—between nine hundred and twelve hundred pounds.

Young donkeys are called foals.

If a male donkey and a female horse have a foal, it is called a mule. If a female donkey and a male horse have a foal, it is called a hinny.

If a donkey and a zebra have a foal, it is called a zonkey.

The "hee-haw" sound that donkeys make is called a bray. Donkeys breathe in on the "hee" and out on the "haw."

Donkeys can be territorial, which means they will drive other animals away from a space they think of as theirs. On a farm, a donkey may drive smaller animals like goats, sheep, dogs, or cats out of its pasture.

READ ON FOR A SNEAK PEEK AT
LILY TO THE RESCUE:
FOXES IN A FIX,
COMING SOON FROM STARSCAPE

I was in a sort of yard. There were two big metal things like trucks parked here, with giant wheels much taller than I was. A hole had been dug in the earth. I like to dig holes, but this one was much bigger than anything I could dig on my own.

There were some piles of rocks, too, and long, thin pieces of wood stacked up in a corner. A small, white face with bright black eyes was peering at me from around that stack of wood.

A friend!

I hurried over to see what games this new friend liked to play, and a little doglike animal tumbled out into the snow. It was white all over, except for its black eyes and nose. And it had a smell that was very much like a dog, but not exactly.

The almost-dog rolled around in the snow. I liked rolling in the snow, too, so I did the same thing. When I rolled over onto my belly, I saw that two more of the almost-dogs had come out from behind the wood pile.

They all smelled like males, and young, too. And they were very good at playing. They knew Chase and Wrestle and Chew-on-Your-Ears and Bite-the-Snow. We raced in a circle and crouched and jumped on each other and ended up in a big wrestling pile, gently gnawing paws and faces and whatever else ended up in our mouths. One almost-dog got my tail and nibbled it gently, so I turned around and sampled his ear.

When I wiggled out of the pile, I glanced around and sniffed. I had a feeling that I was being watched, and sure enough, I could smell more almost-dogs nearby. But it was hard to see them. I spun in a circle and glimpsed one curled up in a hollow next to a rock with his bushy tail over his nose. Another watched alertly from the top of the wood pile.

Just then I heard Maggie Rose calling my name. "Lily, where are you? Lily, come!"

ABOUT THE AUTHOR

W. BRUCE CAMERON is the #1 *New York Times* bestselling author of *A Dog's Purpose*, *A Dog's Journey*, *A Dog's Way Home*, *A Dog's Promise*; the young reader novels *Bailey's Story*, *Bella's Story*, *Ellie's Story*, *Lily's Story*, *Max's Story*, *Molly's Story*, *Shelby's Story*, *Toby's Story*; and the chapter book series Lily to the Rescue. He lives in California.

Don't miss these

LILY TO THE RESCUE

adventures from bestselling author

W. Bruce cameron

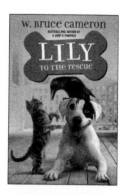

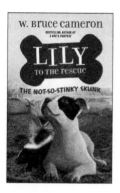

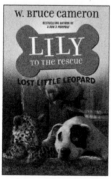

BruceCameronKidsBooks.com